Text Sarah Miller, illustration by Y. La Bunet

BUGSY'S BEST EASTER EVER!

Let's peek into the Bunny family's house
and see what we can see.
Mommy Bunny's baking carrot cake,
the best in the world wouldn't you agree?

Daddy Bunny's great at woodwork
and makes tables, chairs and doors.
He also makes wooden ornaments
and bird tables and bedroom drawers.

Betsy Bunny is the youngest of four
and likes to dance and do ballet.
Beth Bunny is slightly older than Betsy,
she likes to stitch, sew and do crochet.

Brett Bunny is the eldest one of all
and likes to play sports all day long.
His favorites are baseball, hockey,
tennis and a game of ping-pong!

Now Bugsy Bunny is slightly younger
than his older brother Brett.
He loves listening to his music
through his very own headset.

The Bunny family hop happily around,
as it's an exciting time of the year.
Tomorrow is Easter Sunday you see,
when all the yummy chocolate eggs appear.

The bunnies all jump on Brett in a pile.
They laugh and giggle and have fun.
Their mommy looks at her bunnies,
and says, "You'll all find the eggs one by one."

12

One bunny is not with the others,
and he's missing from the rest.
Bugsy is in his room and whispers,
"I will find more eggs and be
better than the rest!"

Later that day, Bugsy visits a friend.
Shirley the squirrel is her name,
and being the best detective
in the whole wide world is her game.

Bugsy knocks upon her cabin's door.
Shirley answers and gives a big grin,
"Hello, my bunny friend Bugsy.
Are you ready to hunt for eggs and win?"

15

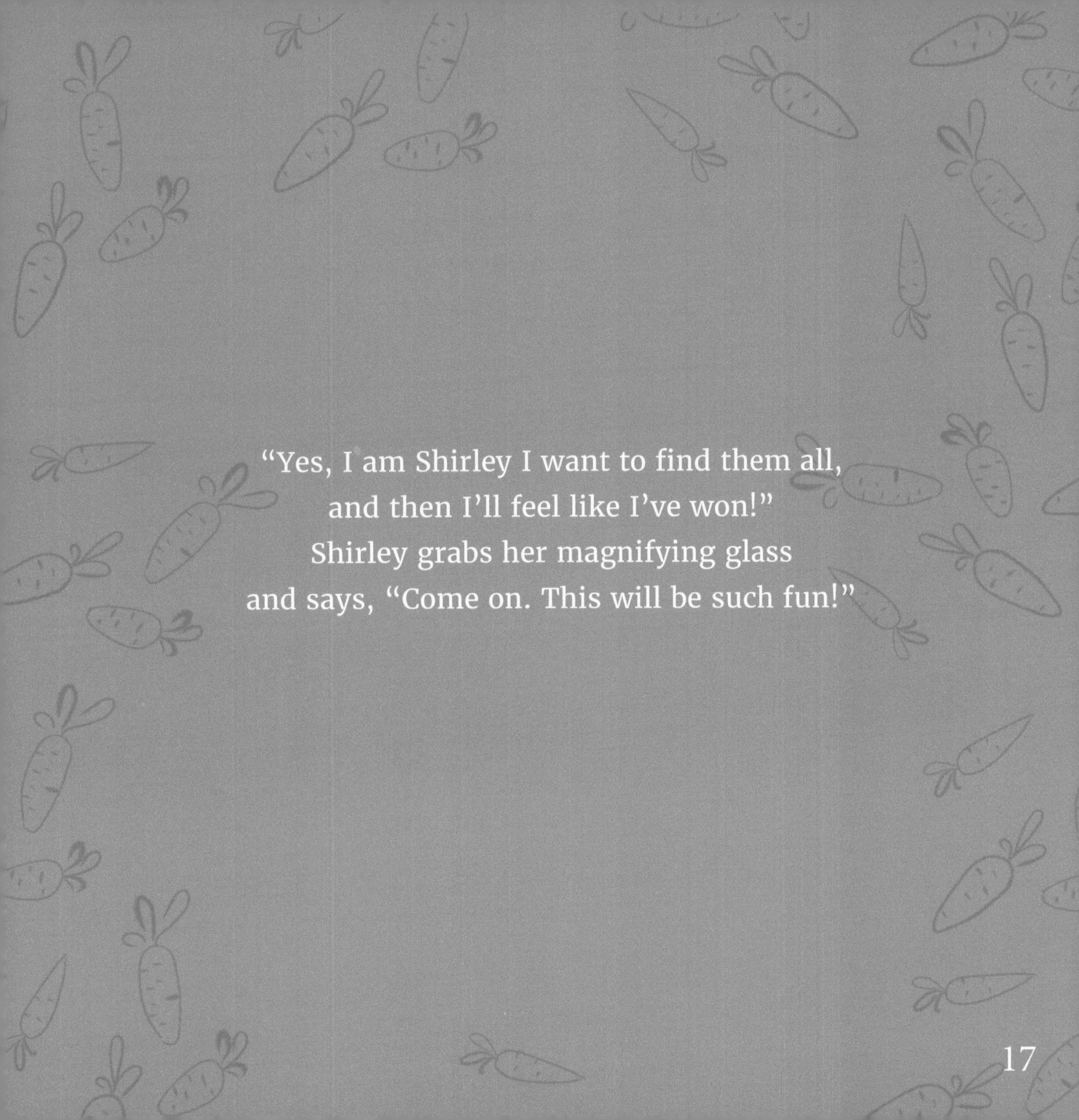

"Yes, I am Shirley I want to find them all,
and then I'll feel like I've won!"
Shirley grabs her magnifying glass
and says, "Come on. This will be such fun!"

They look under a log and there they see,
an Easter egg hidden just out of sight.
"That's one of the SIX eggs found.
Let's find the other FIVE
before the night!"

Bugsy shouts, "LOOK! Shirley up the tree,
another egg with chocolate in white."
"That's the second of the SIX eggs found.
Let's find the other FOUR before the night!"

Bugsy hops into a pile of leaves,
he makes the leaves fly left and right.
"That's the third of the SIX eggs found.
Let's find the other THREE before
the night!"

They find a farm and look in the chicken's house,
Shirley finds the Easter egg amongst all the eggs in white.
"That's the fourth of the SIX eggs found.
Let's find the other TWO before the night!"

20

Bugsy watches as Shirley looks in a hedgehog's hole,
using her magnifying glass to help her eyesight.
"That's the fifth of the SIX eggs found.
Let's find the last ONE before the night!"

The last Easter egg is hard to find.
They search all over and everywhere.
Shirley says, "Look a lot of wooden bee hives,
I wonder if the last Easter egg's there?"

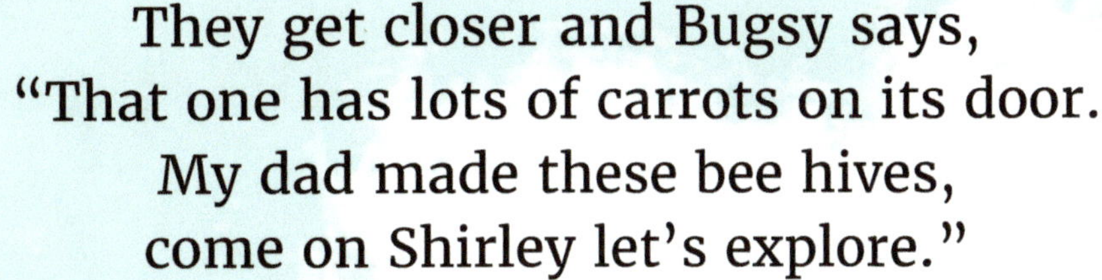

They get closer and Bugsy says,
"That one has lots of carrots on its door.
My dad made these bee hives,
come on Shirley let's explore."

23

Shirley gives a flick of her bushy tail,
and says, "Follow me I'm going to peek,
and take a look for that very last
Easter egg that we seek."

They hug each other and laugh and giggle.
They just can't hide their sheer delight.
"That's the last one of the SIX eggs found.
We found them all before the night!"

Bugsy races home with all the eggs,
to see his brother and sisters looking sad.
Bugsy says, "But I found all the Easter eggs.
Why aren't you all happy and glad?"

Brett and Beth both say at the same time,
"We wanted to join in and find some too.
You took all the fun out of the Easter egg hunt.
The only bunny who had any fun was YOU!"

This made Bugsy feel sad and hurt,
he didn't realize they would feel this way.
He thought they could all play now,
and enjoy this special Easter day.

27

But nobody wanted to play with Bugsy
so, the bunny had nobody to share.
"I've found all these Easter eggs, what do I do?"
He sighs, as he sits down in his chair.

Bugsy realizes how much he loves his family.
He knows he wants to spend time with them all.
Without their love and friendship,
Bugsy feels lonely and small.

Bugsy says, "I'm sorry everyone, let's play.
His family forgives him as that's what families do.
They have fun for the rest of Easter and Bugsy says,
"This has been my best Easter ever, thanks to you!"

HAPPY EASTER!